The Eight-Year-Old Legend Book

# The Eight-Year-Old
# Legend Book

## Isabel Wyatt

### Illustrated by Katriona Chapman

Floris Books

First published in 2009 by Floris Books
Second printing 2011

**Mixed Sources**
Product group from well-managed
forests and other controlled sources
www.fsc.org Cert no. TT-COC-002769
© 1996 Forest Stewardship Council

FSC

British Library CIP Data available

ISBN 978-086315-713-4

Printed in Great Britain
by Bell & Bain Ltd.

The stories in this book are from tales told by the Buddha to his monks 2,500 years ago.

*Out of a world that seems*
*To us today*
*A world of long ago*
*And far away,*
*A world of old, gold dreams,*
*These old, gold stories flow.*
*Yet out of its olden gleams,*
*Out of its golden glow,*
*Into our own time streams*
*The world we know.*
*Out of this ground we grow.*

Isabel Wyatt

# Contents

# The Prince Who Ate Swords

One day a man came running to the city to seek out the king. The king was sitting in his seat, under a white umbrella.

"Sire," the man cried, "a giant has come to our forest!"

The king's son was sitting beside the king.

"What is this giant like?" asked the king's son.

And the man told him, "He is as tall as a palm tree. His eyes are as big as bowls. He has two teeth like parsnips, and a beak like a hawk, and he is covered in long hair."

"Has he a name?" asked the king. For it helps you to fight your foe if you know his name.

"Sire," said the man, "we call him Hairy-Grip. For a thing has only to brush him, and it sticks to his long hair."

"Does he do harm?" asked the king.

"Sire," said the man, "he eats men. No traveller who goes along the forest road is ever seen again."

"I will send my men to kill this giant," said the king.

So the king sent a band of his men to the forest.

They tried to kill Hairy-Grip. They tried with club and dart and sword and spear. But every weapon they had all stuck fast to the giant's long hair.

"Ha-ha!" sang Hairy-Grip. "All the men in all this

land will never kill me. For you will have to get under my hairy skin if you wish to kill me, little men."

Only a few of the king's men came back from that fight with Hairy-Grip. They told the king what the giant had said. The prince sat beside the king's seat and listened.

Now up in the hills, far from the city, a hermit had his hut of reeds and palm fronds. This hermit was very old and very wise.

"Father," said the prince, "I will go up to the hills. I will seek out the hermit. I will ask him to teach me how to get under Hairy-Grip's skin."

So the prince left the city, and went up to the hills. He went to the hut of the hermit and told him all about the giant Hairy-Grip.

"Wise Sir," said the prince, "teach me how to get under the skin of this giant."

"My son," said the hermit, "there is only one way you can get under his skin. That is to let him eat you."

"But how can I kill him then?" cried the prince. "I shall be dead."

"You must first eat a sword," said the hermit. "Then if he eats you, the sword inside you will chop him into bits."

The prince stood still to think. He did not wish to die. But he did wish to rid his father's land of Hairy-Grip.

At last he said, "Wise Sir, if this is the only way, so be it. Teach me how to eat swords." And the hermit did so.

The prince learned how to eat a sword in such a way

that it did him no harm. Then he took another sword and hung it at his side. On his back he hung his dart case, with fifty darts in it. In his right hand he took his club, and in his left hand he held his spear.

"First I will try to kill him in open fight," he told the hermit.

But the hermit said, "It is not good to take life — not even the life of a giant who eats men. Now that you can eat swords, I think you may find out a way to send him back to his own land, and so rid this land of him. And in his own land he will do no more harm."

"I will try to do this, Wise Sir," said the prince.

Then he left the hut of the hermit, and went down from the hills to the plain, and across the plain to the forest.

All the men he met along the road said to him, "Sir, do not go into the forest. For there lives the giant Hairy-Grip. And he eats all the men he meets."

But the prince told them, "I shall send him back to his own land." And on he went, into the forest.

In the forest, the prince met the giant Hairy-Grip. He was as tall as a palm tree; his eyes were as big as bowls; he had two big teeth like parsnips, and a beak like a hawk's; and he was covered in long hair.

Hairy-Grip stood still when he saw the prince. "Come here, little man," he cried, "so that I can eat you!"

"First I will fight you, Hairy-Grip," said the prince. And he cast a dart at the giant. The dart stuck fast on Hairy-Grip's hairy skin.

One by one, the prince cast all his fifty darts at Hairy-Grip. They all stuck fast on the giant's hairy skin. Then Hairy-Grip shook his arms and legs. All the darts fell, and lay at his feet.

Now the prince came three steps closer, and cast his spear at Hairy-Grip. The spear stuck fast on the giant's hairy skin.

The prince came forward three more steps, and flung his club at Hairy-Grip, but the club stuck fast.

The prince came three steps closer still, and swung his sword at Hairy-Grip, but the sword stuck fast.

The giant shook his arms and legs. The spear and the club and the sword all fell off, and lay at his feet.

The prince took three more steps; and now he was right up to the giant. He gave Hairy-Grip a good blow with his right fist and then with his left fist, but both hands stuck fast to the hairy skin.

The prince gave Hairy-Grip a good kick with his right foot, and then with his left foot, but both feet stuck fast to the hairy skin.

Last of all, the prince gave Hairy-Grip a butt with the top of his head. But the top of his head stuck fast to the giant's hairy skin.

All this time, the giant just stood there. And now the prince was stuck fast to him by his hands and his feet and his head.

"Now I shall eat you, little man," said Hairy-Grip.

"Yes, do eat me, Hairy-Grip," said the prince. "For then I can kill you, for I shall be under your skin."

"It is true you will be under my skin, little man," said Hairy-Grip. "But how will you kill me?"

And the prince told him, "I have a sword in me that will chop you into bits."

"That is not true," said Hairy-Grip. "No man has a sword in him."

"Look in my mouth and you'll see," said the prince. So Hairy-Grip freed the prince's head. The prince held up his face, with his mouth wide open.

The giant bent down to look. He saw the top of a sword hilt in the prince's throat. Then Hairy-Grip, in fear of his life, cried out, "Little man, I will not eat you. I will let you go."

"But I will not let *you* go," said the prince, "till you promise you'll go back to your own land and stay there."

"But if I do that," said Hairy-Grip, "I shall have no more men to eat."

"That is exactly why you must go," said the prince.

"I will not go back," said Hairy-Grip. "Didn't you see me shake off all your darts? I will shake you off, too."

He tried to shake the prince off. But the prince clung fast to him.

At last Hairy-Grip cried, "Let me go, little man. I promise I'll go back to my own land, and eat no more men and do no more harm as long as I live."

Then the prince tore his right foot free from Hairy-Grip, and then his left foot, and stood on his own two feet on the grass. Then he tore his right hand free, and then his left hand.

And as soon as the prince was free, Hairy-Grip left the forest and went back to his own land. He never did any more harm, and he never ate any more men.

And the prince who ate swords went back to the city, and sat peacefully beside the king under his white umbrella.

# How Milk-White Flew

Men once sent a message to a king to tell him that they had seen a milk-white elephant in the jungle. White elephants were rare; and it was the wish of all kings to have one.

The king sent a message back to say, "Catch her, and send her to me. If she is as white as you say, I will pay you well for her."

So the men dug a pit in the path that the white elephant took when she went to drink. On her way to the river she fell into the pit; and the men took her out, and sent her to the king.

She was everything that the men claimed she would be. Her trunk was like a silver rope, and her skin was as white as a lotus stem.

The king said to her oozie, the elephant-man who was to take care of her, "Train her well, for I wish to make her my state elephant."

The oozie was a good elephant-man. He was gentle and kind, and Milk-White grew to love him. What the oozie told her to do, Milk-White always did.

He had to train her to wear rich cloths on her back, and gold and gems on her trunk, when the king rode into the city on feast days. He had to train her not to mind the crowds in the streets, and the shouts and the harsh beat of the drums.

But he also had to train her to wear armour when

the king rode out to war. He had to train her how to go mad when he told her to, and to charge among the king's foes.

Milk-White and her oozie had special names for some of the things he trained her to do. Once he said to her, "Milk-White, why do you charge when you sniff the south wind?"

And she told him, "When I sniff the south wind, trumpets sound in my mind, and the hills and the sky swing to and fro, and I seem to fly. That is why I charge."

After that, when he wanted her to charge, he always cried, "Fly, Milk-White."

Milk-White's fame grew far and wide. The king of the next land begged Milk-White's king to sell her to him, for his own state elephant had died. But Milk-White's king said, "No. I shall keep her. Milk-White is mine."

Yet as time went on, the king grew to hate Milk-White. She was so beautiful and so well trained that all the city fell in love with her.

When the king rode out on her on feast days, with his white umbrella, the crowds ran to gaze. But they all cried, "Look at Milk-White!" No-one cried, "Look at the king!"

At last the king went mad with spite and rage. He said in his own mind, "Milk-White must die!"

And so the king set about trying to find a way to kill Milk-White. At last he realized, "Milk-White will do just what her oozie tells her. *That* is how I will bring about her death!"

Now above the city was a flat hilltop. The way up was a gentle slope; but on the other side it dropped steeply. So the king sent men into all the streets of the city to cry out, with beat of drum, "Come to the cliff edge at the Feast of the Full Moon. Milk-White will dance for you."

The city was excited by the news; and on the day of the Feast of the Full Moon, the crowds went up to the cliff edge, just like ants swarming up a tree trunk.

Milk-White came up the hill, clad in rich silks, with gold and gems glittering on her trunk. She bore the king on her back, and her oozie sat by her ear. The crowd sent up cheer after cheer as they made way for her to pass.

The hilltop was so full that the only space left for Milk-White was near the edge of the cliff. As she approached the edge, the king slid down from her back, and stood in front of the crowds.

"Let Milk-White stand on two legs," said the king to the oozie.

"Stand on two legs, Milk-White," said the oozie in her ear.

Milk-White stood on two legs at the edge of the cliff. First she stood on her two front legs; then on her two hind legs; then on her two right legs; then on her two left legs.

"Milk-White! Milk-White!" cried the crowd. And they gave cheer after cheer.

"Let Milk-White dance," said the king to the oozie.

"Dance, Milk-White," said the oozie in her ear.

Milk-White began to dance at the edge of the cliff. To and fro, and in and out, and round and round she went, her big ears raised up like white wings, and her silver trunk swaying.

"Milk-White! Milk-White!" cried the crowd. And again they gave cheer after cheer.

"Let Milk-White fly," said the king to the oozie.

"Fly, Milk-White," said the oozie in her ear.

Now the king's plan was for Milk-White to step off the edge of the cliff, and so dash down to her death. He did not know that when her oozie told Milk-White to fly, she charged.

She charged now. Round she swung from the edge of the cliff. Stamp, stamp, tramp, tramp, went her feet.

Down under her huge feet went the king. The crowd fled this way, that way, with cries of fear. Down the hill went Milk-White at full speed, her oozie still at her ear.

"You are too good for this bad king, Milk-White," said her oozie. "He must be mad. It was in his mind to kill you. The king of the next land longs for you; let us go to him."

So on ran Milk-White, and she did not stop until they came to the next king's city. He took them in with joy; and when the men of his land, too, fell in love with Milk-White, he was glad of it. With this kind king Milk-White and her oozie lived long lives in joy and peace.

# The Lame Cat and the Potter

There was a poor potter who made pots out of clay. One day he went out into the wood to get sticks to make a fire to bake his pots. He saw two wise men go by.

A dead rat was lying in the mud. The potter saw the two wise men stop and look at the rat. One said to the other, "A poor man who has pity has only to pick up that rat and he will grow rich."

"Yes," said the other, "and he will get a wife who is good and lovely, too."

Then the two wise men went on.

The potter put down his sticks and ran to pick up the dead rat. As he stood with it in his hand, a little lame cat came by, with her tail in the air.

When she saw the dead rat, she said, with a sad little mew, "Wise-Man Potter, if you will give me that rat, you will save my life. You can see I am too lame to hunt for my food; and if I do not eat soon, I shall die."

The potter felt such pity for the little lame cat that he held out the rat to her. She took it in her claws and ate it all up. Then she said, "And now, Wise-Man Potter, I can help *you*."

First, she led him back to his hut, with her tail in the air.

"Bring out all your water pots, Wise-Man Potter," she said.

The potter did as the lame cat told him.

Then she led him to the river, with her tail in the air.

"Fill your water pots with this ice-cold water, Wise-Man Potter," she said.

The potter did as the lame cat told him.

Then she led him back into the wood, with her tail in the air. But she led him to a part of the wood that was new to him. She led him to a cliff that was hung with the wax nests of bees. The air all about it was sweet with the smell of honey.

"Add some of this honey to your ice-cold water, Wise-Man Potter," the lame cat said.

The potter did as the lame cat told him.

Then she led him to a vast grass patch, with her tail in the air. In the grass patch were ranks and ranks of men; they all swung scythes to cut down the grass and left it to dry in the hot sun.

"Let the men drink from your water pots, Wise-Man Potter," the lame cat said.

The potter did as the lame cat told him. The men were glad to stop, and to stand up, and to rest for a little, and to drink deep of the cold, sweet water.

"But we have no money," they told the potter. "So how can we pay you?"

The little lame cat stood by, with her tail in the air.

"Ask them each to put a sack of grass by the wall of your hut when they go home at dusk," she said.

The potter did as the lame cat told him. And at dusk each of the men, as he went home, left a sack of his grass by the wall of the potter's hut.

At dawn, the little lame cat again led the potter to the river, with her tail in the air. He saw a ship slide up the river and glide to rest by the riverbank. He saw it was one of the king's ships.

As the men tied the ship fast, he asked them, "What do you bring for the king this time?"

"Mares for his stable," they told him.

They let down the gangway and led the mares to land. Then they said to the potter, "We have run out of grass for the mares. Can you tell us who will sell us some?"

"I will," said the potter. "Come with me."

And the little lame cat led them back to his hut, with her tail in the air.

The potter sold all his sacks of grass to the king's men for the king's mares. For his sacks of grass they gave him a sack of gold.

Then the potter said to the little lame cat, "I got all this gold for that dead rat, Lame Cat. Thank you. But now I must find the two wise men who told me about the rat, and thank them, too."

"I will take you to them, Wise-Man Potter," said the little lame cat.

And off she set, with her tail in the air.

She led him to the city, and in at the city gate, and along the city streets, with her tail in the air.

She led him at last to the two wise men, and he told them both his tale, and he gave them both his thanks.

"What shall I do with all this gold, Wise Sirs?" he asked them.

"Give it to me," said one. "I will put it into a ship for you; when your cargo is sold in some far land, your gold will grow into more, and with that you can get a new cargo that will make it grow still more."

"And I," said the other wise man, "will make you my son-in-law. I shall be glad to have a son who has so much sense and at the same time so much pity."

So the poor potter grew rich, and had a wife as good as she was lovely, just as the two wise men had said when they had first seen the dead rat in the mud. The little lame cat with her tail in the air went to live with them. And all three of them lived happy ever after.

# The King's Friend

There was a king who needed rare trees to decorate the garden of his new palace. So he sent his men out into the jungle to find trees for him.

As they came to each one, they put the king's mark on it, and told the tree that they must pull it up, but that first the king would come to burn spices in front of it.

The next day the king went to do this. His raft took him up the river to the jungle. As he went from tree to tree, he saw an elephant limping after him. At last, the elephant lay down in the king's path, and held up his left hind foot to him.

The king knelt down by the elephant, and took the foot in his hand to look at it. He saw that a long thorn had pierced it and made it swollen. He pulled out the thorn, and told his men to warm water for him to bathe the foot with.

In a day or two the foot was better and the elephant went from tree to tree with the king to show his thanks. He helped the king's men to pull up trees, or to roll logs, or to hold tools in his trunk for them.

And he went to the men's small sons to play with them in the river. He let them ride on his back, and pull him by the trunk, and play all sorts of games with him.

When the king had visited all the trees that were

to be taken, his raft came again up the river to carry him back to the city. The elephant stood on the river-bank and cast a last look round at the jungle. Then, of his own free will, he stepped on to the raft with the king.

When the raft arrived at the city, the king rode the elephant in at the gates; and from all parts of the city men ran to see the elephant who had come with the king of his own free will.

The king rode the elephant to his own elephant sta-ble, and made his mark on his brow with oil. He made him his own state elephant; and they grew to be as dear to each other as a father and a son.

The king had the elephant fed on three-year-old rice from a golden dish. He had the elephant's stall hung with gay red cloths and its roof set with golden stars. Each day he had fresh garlands hung on its posts; and each dusk he had a rose-red lamp lit in the stable to burn all night.

And he gave out the announcement that the ele-phant was always to be known by the name of the King's Friend.

Then one day the king fell sick and died.

Even in the midst of her own grief, the queen did not forget the King's Friend. She was not able to go to him then, for a son had just been born to her. But she sent to the elephant-men to say, "The King's Friend will pine with grief if he hears the king is dead. So keep the news from him till I can come to him."

So they kept the news from the King's Friend.

When the news of the king's death came to the king

of the next land, he said, "That land has no king to fight for it. Now is the time for me to take it for my own."

So he went with a host of his men to take the city.

The queen had the gate of the city shut to keep them out. But she had no-one to send to lead the king's men into battle.

"The time has come; the King's Friend must be told," she said.

So she wrapped a fine shawl around her small son, and carried him out to the stall of the King's Friend.

She laid the child at his feet and said, "King's Friend, we have sad news that we did not tell you till now, lest it broke your heart. The king your friend is dead. But see the son who has been born to him; and let this son be *your* son too."

The King's Friend put out his trunk to feel the child, and then to lift him towards his own eyes. Then he let him down and laid him in the queen's arms.

The queen went on, "King's Friend, the king of the next land has come to take our city. Will you help your son to keep it? I have no-one else to send out at the head of his men."

The King's Friend let out a trumpet-blare to request that his war-mail was brought to him. The stablemen ran to get his armour and put it on him. Then they opened wide the gates of the city.

Out went the King's Friend.

He gave a loud trumpet-call as he ran: "Ho, all you elephants, ho! A bad king has led you here! Do not help him to take this land from my small son! Charge! Charge!"

And all the elephants in the ranks of the enemy turned and charged towards those who had come to take the city, so that they fled in fear.

Then the King's Friend went back amid the glad

cries of his people. And he kept the land safe for the little king until he grew up.

And just as the old king had been as dear to him as a father, so the new king grew to be as dear to him as a son.

# The Ape-king

A fig tree once grew on the bank of a wide river. The tree was as tall as a hill. Its figs were as big as water jars.

A tribe of apes lived in the jungle nearby. The name of the ape-king was Kapi.

As the figs on the fig tree grew ripe, the apes came often to feed on them. On one side of the tree, the ripe figs fell on dry land. On the other side, they fell into the river.

Kapi said to his apes, "My dears, if we let a ripe fig fall into the water, it will bring us bad luck. Do not let them get ripe on that side."

So the apes went to the end of each long branch that hung over the river. They broke off all the green figs and threw them all away.

But one green fig they did not see, for an ant nest clung to it and hid it. So this fig hung on until it was ripe.

Then it fell, and the ant nest fell with it.

Now the king of that land did not take much care of his land and the men who lived in it. He just ate and drank and was merry, and did not think a king had a duty to his people.

One day, this king went out to play games in the river. He had a net under him and a net over him. And when the ripe fig in its ant nest fell, it landed on the king's top net and hung in its mesh.

At dusk, the king left the river and went back to his city. When his boatmen took in the nets, they saw the ripe fig in its ant nest.

They took it to the king.

"What is it?" he asked.

"Sire, it is a ripe fig in an ant nest," they told him.

The king cut it, and ate a bit of it. It was so sweet that he said, "Can you take me to the tree this fell from?"

"Sire, we can," the boatmen said.

"Then let us go," replied the king.

"Now, Sire?" cried the men. "At dusk?"

"Yes, now, at dusk," said the king. "I must find out at once if all the figs on that tree are as sweet as this one is."

So the boatmen took the king back by river to the fig tree. He left the boat and broke off figs and ate them. They were just as sweet as the first.

"We will spend the night under this fig tree," said the king. "And at dawn we will strip the tree of all its figs, and fill the boat with them."

So the boatmen lit a fire near the fig tree. And the king lay down and slept by it. And the boatmen, too, lay down and slept, a little way away.

Soon the fire died down to a glow, and all was still in the king's camp. Then the ape-king and his apes came to feed in the fig tree.

"Eat your fill, my dears," Kapi told them. "For at dawn this king will strip the tree bare. But take care not to wake him."

The apes made no noise as they sprang from branch

to branch. But the branch that hung over the king shook as an ape sprang on it; and *plop*, a ripe fig fell on the king's face.

The king woke up with a start. He put up his hand and felt the fig. The apes sat still as stones in the dark fig tree.

The king cried out to the boatmen, "Put more wood on the fire!"

The boatmen sprang up, and ran to put wood on the fire. When they did so, a flame shot up and lit up the fig tree, and the king saw the apes above him.

He said to two of the boatmen, "Go to the city and bring back my bowmen."

And to the rest he said, "Stand in a ring around the tree to stop the apes from escaping. At dawn, as soon as my bowmen can see, they shall shoot them all, and we can all have ape flesh to eat."

The boatmen stood in a ring around the fig tree. The apes in the tree felt sick with fear.

"What shall we do?" they cried. "At dawn we shall be shot!"

"Be still, my dears," said Kapi. "I will find a way to save you."

"How can you?" they cried. "We are cut off by land. And we do not swim."

"If we can leap the river, we shall be safe," said Kapi.

"The river is too wide," said the rest of the apes. "You are so big, King Kapi, that maybe you can leap it. But it is too far for the rest of us to jump."

"A bamboo clump grows on the other side," said Kapi. "I will try to make a bamboo bridge for you to cross the river."

A long branch of the fig tree hung out over the water. This was the branch from which the ripe fig in its ant nest had hung.

Kapi crept to the end of the branch. Then he sprang a long, strong spring into the dark.

He landed on his feet in the bamboo clump on the far side of the river. On the bank just above him he saw the black bulk of a tree. A long vine hung from it.

Kapi broke off a tall bamboo shoot at its root. He found a long branch of the tree that hung over the river. Using the vine for string, he tied one end of the bamboo shoot to the end of this branch.

The other end of the bamboo shoot he tied to his own leg. Then again he sprang his long, strong spring back over the river and out into the dark.

Kapi's plan was to leap back into the fig tree, and to tie his end of the bamboo shoot to the fig tree's long branch.

But alas, the bamboo shoot was too short and the river too wide. He was just able to reach out and clutch the end of the long branch as he fell.

As he clung to the branch, he hung flat in the air. If he was to save his apes, *he* must be part of the bridge.

So now he said to them, "Pass over my back and on to the bamboo shoot. Be as swift as you can, my dears."

In a long, long line his apes ran over his back and along the bamboo shoot, and then into the tree on the far bank of the river. Kapi hung and clung to the long fig branch until all were safe on the other side.

It took a long, long time. His arms and legs felt as if they would be torn out.

The king of the land had seen all this by the red flame of the fire. The two boatmen had arrived back

with his bowmen, and they stood now with bows all strung.

"Shall we shoot, Sire?" they asked. "If we wait till dawn, they will all be out of reach."

But the king said to his bowmen, "No, do not shoot."

And to his boatmen he said, "Heap the boat with soft cloths."

The boatmen did so. Then the king rose and got into the boat.

"Push the boat out from the bank. Stop when it is just under the ape-king," he ordered.

Again the boatmen did so.

Then the king cried to Kapi, as he hung in pain in the dark over his head, "Let go your hold of the fig branch now, Kapi. All your apes are safe on the far bank. The boat is full of soft cloths for you to fall on."

And Kapi let go his hold of the fig branch, and fell with a thud on the heap of soft cloths in the boat. He felt stiff and sore and faint. He lay still like a log.

The king cut the vine that tied Kapi's leg to the bamboo shoot. He set his men to wash away the blood and to rub the ape-king with oil. He fed him with ripe figs. He held water in his hands for him to drink.

The king kept Kapi with him till he felt strong again. Then he took him in the boat to the far side of the river, and set him down on the bank among his apes.

"If a king of apes can do this for his apes," he said, "a king of men must do no less for his people."

And from that day on, he was a wise and good king, and he took care of his land and of all those who lived in it.

# The Sneeze that Won a Wife

There was a king who had a son who was in love with the princess of the next land, and she with him. But her father did not wish her to marry this prince, so he kept her shut up in his palace.

The prince tried to find a way to steal the princess from her father. But he did not find one — until one day his gaze fell on his father's sword-tester.

Now every time a swordsmith made a sword, the sword-tester would put it to his nose to sniff. If the smith gave him a big bribe, he would say the sword was a good one. If the smith gave him no bribe, he would not pass the sword.

One day a swordsmith gave a new blade to the sword-tester to be tested. But he gave him no bribe, so the sword-tester did not pass the sword.

The smith went straight back to his smithy and made a second sword. He slid it into its sheath, and in the sheath he put pepper. Then he took the sword to the sword-tester.

The sword-tester drew the blade out and put it to his nose to sniff. But the pepper on the sword made him sneeze and jerk the sword up, so that he cut off the end of his nose.

He had a new tip for his nose made out of clay. And with a dab of paint it looked just like a real nose. But from then on, he did not test swords any more.

Now the prince, seeing the sword-tester's nose, found that a plan was forming in his mind. He took gold and pepper and a swift steed. And off he rode to the city where his princess was locked away by her father.

The prince sat down by the river, near the spot where the women of the city went to collect water. Soon he saw his princess's nurse coming along the track, with a water jar on her head.

As she bent down to fill the water jar, the prince took out a purse and held it out to her. She took it, and drew the string. She saw that it was full of gold.

"And what am I to do with this?" she asked.

"Nurse, look at me," said the prince. "Do you not know me?"

The old nurse stared hard at him.

"Why, you are the prince my princess is in love with!" she cried. "But try as hard as you will, you will not see her. The king keeps her locked away."

"With your help I shall see her," the prince told her. "Tell me, in this land how do you drive out a demon?"

"We take the man to the king's park by night," she said, "and lay him on the stone seat by the gate, and say a spell over him; and the spell drives the demon out."

"That is how we do it in *my* land, too," said the prince. "So you must tell the princess to be sick, Nurse, and then tell the king she has a demon."

"That will not help you," said the nurse. "For even if he sends her to his park for me to drive the demon out, he will send his men with her."

"I shall hide under the stone slab of the bench," said

the prince. "When I sneeze, you must take to your heels. You must get the king's men to do the same."

"Aha, now I see!" said the nurse. "It is a good plan. Yes, I can do it."

And back to the palace she went, with her full water jar on her head.

The old nurse went at once to the princess.

"Princess," she said, "I have seen your prince. He has come to take you away."

"But how?" cried the princess.

"With a sneeze," said the nurse.

And she told the princess the plan that the prince had told her.

"I am sick. Put me to bed, Nurse!" said the princess, full of joy.

The old nurse put her to bed. Then she went to the king.

"Sire," she said, "the princess is sick. I have put her to bed. I fear she has a demon."

"Let me come and see her," said the king.

He came and stood by the bed of the princess. When she saw him come into the room, she began to toss and turn, and to rave, and to cry out in a speech that she made up as she went along.

"Yes," said the king. "You are right, Nurse. She has a demon. You must take her to my park as soon as it is dark, and say a spell to drive the demon out of her."

"But, Sire, is it safe to let the princess go out?" asked the old nurse.

"Safe? Why not?" cried the king. "I shall send my men with you."

Then the old nurse went to the king's men and said to them, "Take care when we are in the park. The demon will sneeze as he flies out of the princess. Then he will go into the first man he finds. So you must all keep well out of his way!"

"You can trust us to do that," said the men.

As soon as it was dark, the prince hid under the stone bench by the gate of the king's park. He hid his swift steed in the trees nearby. But his pepper he took with him.

Soon the king's men came, carrying the princess and her old nurse on a couch. They laid the princess on the stone bench, and the old nurse stood at her side.

"Stand back," said the nurse to the men, "and take care when you hear the demon sneeze."

She said the spell over the princess; and when she got to the end, the prince took a deep, deep sniff at his pepper. The sneeze he gave was so loud that all the king's men shook with fear and fled for dear life.

Then out came the prince from under the bench.

"Quick, to your horse!" cried the nurse. "I shall ride with you — on the best steed from the king's stable!"

The prince lifted the princess up on to his horse, and all three rode all night. At dawn they came to the city of the prince's father, and were made man and wife.

In time, the old king died, and the prince was made king in his place. He kept the sword-tester about him, and gave him a good place at court. Sometimes, when it was very hot, the tip of the sword-tester's nose began to melt, and he hung his head in shame.

But the prince would cry out to him, "Never mind! For some a sneeze brings bad luck, for some it brings good luck. A sneeze lost you your nose, but for me it won my wife. For that I have you to thank; so your sneeze may bring you good luck yet."

"Only," added the king, "do not take bribes any more."

And the sword-tester did not, but was a wise and honest man from then on.

# Prince Bowman

There was a king who had two sons who were twins. One was the best bowman ever seen in all the land. From this he got the name of Prince Bowman.

On his deathbed, the old king said, "When I die Prince Bowman should be commander of all my armies, and his brother should be king."

So when the old king died, the two sons did as he had said.

So much did Prince Bowman's men love him that the new queen said to the new king, "My lord, do not trust your brother. His men love him too much. What if they kill you, and make him king in your place?"

The king sat down to think about this. At last he said, "Lady dear, you are right. It is best that I kill him first."

And he sent his men to kill Prince Bowman.

But they, too, were fond of the prince. They came to him and said, "Prince Bowman, the king your brother has sent us to kill you. Flee, we beg you, and we will tell him we came too late."

"Can this be true?" cried Prince Bowman. "*Why* did the king send you?"

"He fears that you will kill him," they told him, "so that *you* can be king."

"I will go and tell him this is not so," said Prince Bowman.

"As long as you stay in the land, the queen will not rest," they told him. "The king will try to take your life some other way. Go now; that is best."

Then Prince Bowman saw they were right; and he fled from the land.

Now the prince was in love with the princess of the next land. So, to be near her, he went to that land, but as a bowman, not as a prince. And he went to ask the king, her father, if he had need of a bowman.

When he came to this king, he was in his park, sitting on a bench, with the princess at his side.

"Yes, I have need of a bowman if he is able," said the king. "Show me your skill."

The bench was under a tall mango tree, and at the top of this tree hung a big bunch of mango fruit.

"Shall I bring down those mangoes with my bow, Sire?" he asked.

"Do, if you can," said the king.

Prince Bowman took his bowcase from his back, and took out his bow of ram's horn, with its bowstring as red as coral. He took off his white robe, and stood up in only his turban and his red undercloth.

"Sire," he said, "do you wish the bunch cut off with an upshot, or by an arrow in its fall?"

"I have never seen one cut off by an arrow in its fall," replied the king. "That must need much skill. Do it that way, if you can."

"That will need two arrows," said Prince Bowman.

He let his first arrow fly; and up it went into the sky. The next arrow was still more swift. It struck the first, so that this one fell back. It cleft the air like a thunderbolt. It cut the mango bunch clean off its stem.

Down came both arrows; down came the mango bunch. Prince Bowman put down his bow and stood with both hands held out, the left hand to catch the arrows, the right hand to catch the mangoes.

He laid the mangoes at the feet of the princess. And all who had seen Prince Bowman's skill began to cheer, and to clap hands and wave gay cloths in the air.

"I think only one man in all the land can show such skill," said the king. "Can it be that you are Prince Bowman?"

"Sire, I am," said Prince Bowman.

"Then you shall stay with me," said the king, "not as my bowman, but as my son. You shall marry my only child; and when I die, you shall be king of this land after me."

"But, Father," cried the princess, "what of my vow? The prince is a bowman; he may not wish such a vow to bind him."

"Lady, tell me your vow," said Prince Bowman.

And she told him, "My vow is that I will only marry a man who from then on will shed no blood, not even as much as a tiny fly can sip."

"Lady, that vow shall bind me," said Prince Bowman.

So the king gave the princess to Prince Bowman as his wife; and for a time they lived with him in joy.

Now in time the news came to the nearby kingdoms that Prince Bowman had left the land of his brother. And so seven of the kings met, and made a pact to go to war and win that land, and then to share it among them.

"It will not be hard to win that land," they said, "now that Prince Bowman has left. The king his brother is not brave; he will fear to fight seven of us."

So the seven kings went with seven armies to take the city. The king shut the gates of the city, and was half-dead with fear.

"Ah, how I need my brother now!" he cried.

And he sent men to Prince Bowman. "Go, fall at his feet in my name," he told them. Beg him to come back with all haste to save the land from my foes."

Prince Bowman sent a reply to say, "I will come."

"But what of the vow that binds you?" cried the princess. "How can you save the city when you must shed no blood, not even as much as a tiny fly may sip?"

"Lady dear," said Prince Bowman, "I will keep the vow. And yet I will save the city."

Prince Bowman went back to his own land. The news ran all round the city: "Prince Bowman! Prince Bowman is back!"

Then roar after roar of joy went up all over the city, till all the seven kings and all the men in the seven armies began to ask each other, "What can it be? Why is this city so glad?"

Prince Bowman took a palm leaf and a tool to scratch it with. On it he wrote, "This is to tell you that I, Prince Bowman, am back. I can shoot the spears from your hands and the food from your lips. The way this will reach you will show you what I can do. Flee, then; for at dawn I shall start."

Then he went up on the arch over the main gate of the city, and he looked down upon the seven kings as they sat eating around a golden dish.

He tied the palm leaf to an arrow, and he took his bow, and he shot the arrow so that it fell into the golden dish.

They took the palm leaf off the arrow, and read it.

And at once the news ran all round the seven camps: "Prince Bowman! Prince Bowman is back!"

By dawn next day, all seven kings had fled, and all the seven armies with them.

Then Prince Bowman went back to his wife and told her, "Lady dear, I kept the vow. I shed no blood, not even as much as a tiny fly can sip."

And by this skill with the bow he kept peace in his land all the rest of his life.

# Monkey Fat

There was once a king who kept a wise man in his court to advise him. When the wise man died it came to the ears of a very lazy man indeed. He said to himself, "The king will need a new wise man to help him rule the land well. I will dress like a sage and go to him. If he will take me to be his new sage, I shall be set up for life."

In the old days, a sage wore a yellow robe, and grew his hair long, and did it up in a top-knot. So the lazy man put on a yellow robe and tied a false top-knot on top of his head. Then he went to the king.

"Sire, you have lost your sage," he said. "Shall I take his place?"

"Wise Sir," said the king, "first stay with me till I find out how wise you are."

So the false sage went to live in the palace of the king till the time came to test him.

One day, the false sage went out to the king's park to bathe in the lotus pond. In the pond, he took off his false top-knot to wash his head.

Now a troop of monkeys lived in the trees in the king's park. One of the monkeys was near the pond when the false sage took off his false top-knot, and he saw him do it.

The monkey got some long grass and made it into a false top-knot that he tied on top of his own head.

Then he began to strut up and down with the lame step of the false sage.

All the rest of the monkeys ran up to see what he was doing. They cried out to him, "Tell *us* this new game. Let *us* play it too."

And the first monkey told them, "I am pretending to be that lazy man. He must be a false sage, for he has a false top-knot. I just saw him take it off to wash his head."

So all the monkeys got long grass and made false top-knots and tied them on. They all began to strut up and down with the step of the false sage.

When the false sage came out of the lotus pond, he saw the monkeys at their new game. And he knew at once that *he* was the man they were mocking.

"If the king sees this, I will be ruined," he said. "I must find a way to stop them. The only way is to get rid of all the monkeys in the park. Now how can I do that?"

And this was in his mind all the way back to the palace.

Now at dusk that day, a girl sat in the street to grind rice. At her back was the wall of the palace courtyard. As it grew dark, she lit a torch to see by, and stuck it in the wall at her side.

A stray goat came up, and began to eat the rice as fast as she ground it. She sent him off with a shout and a slap of her hand again and again. But still the goat came back to eat more of her rice.

At last the girl took the torch in her hand, and gave the goat a whack with that. The torch set the hair of the goat on fire. He ran to a hut nearby and rubbed his back on the wall of the hut to try to put the fire out. But the hut was made of grass, and at once it went up in flames.

Now the hut was near the king's elephant stables, and the wind was blowing towards them. Soon the stables, too, were on fire.

The king's men ran with water. It did not take them long to put the fire out, but the backs of some of the elephants were burned.

The king sent for his elephant doctors to heal the burns with ointments. But the cure was slow, and the elephants began to go mad with pain.

The king said to the false sage, "Wise Sir, the time has come for you to help me. Can you tell me a swift cure for elephant burns?"

The false sage said in his own mind, "Now is my time to get rid of the monkeys in the king's park."

To the king he said, "Sire, I can. Rub them with monkey fat. This cure is both swift and sure."

"But how can I get monkey fat?" asked the king. "I shall need so much to heal so many elephants."

"Sire," said the false sage, "your park is full of monkeys. Send your bowmen to kill all they can find."

"Yes, that will be best," said the king.

So he sent for his bowmen. He told the head bowman, "Go to my park. Kill all the monkeys you can find. Take the monkey fat to my elephant doctors for them to rub on the elephants' burns."

The bowmen took bows and arrows, and went out to where the path ran along by the wall of the park. At the sound of the bowmen's feet, the king of the monkeys sprang to the top of the wall to see who went by.

When he saw the bowmen halt at the gate of the park, he said to his monkey scouts, "My dears, I do not like the look of this. What else but us can they kill in the king's park? Go and tell the rest of our band to flee at once into the jungle. I will stay and find out what this is all about; and when it is safe for you to return, I will come and fetch you."

So all the monkeys fled to the jungle. Only the monkey-king was left. He hid in a safe lair of his own.

The bowmen went to and fro among the trees with drawn bows to shoot the monkeys. But they did not find one monkey to shoot in all the park.

At last the head bowman said, "The king's sage said the park was full of monkeys. They must have all fled. We shall go back and tell the king we can get no monkey fat here for his elephants."

And back the bowmen went to the city to tell the king.

"So that's it, is it?" said the monkey-king. "The false sage knows that we know he is a false sage, so he plots to kill us. I will not let him do that. I will find a way to let the king know he is a false sage. Then he will be sure to send him away, and my monkeys will be safe."

So he went to the gate of the king's park, and sprang up and sat on top of the arch.

When the bowmen got back to the city, they went to the king. He asked them, "How much monkey fat did you get for my elephants?"

And the head bowman told him, "Sire, we got none. We did not find one monkey in all your park."

Then the king said to the false sage, "How can that be? Did you not say that my park was full of monkeys?"

"I did, Sire. It was," replied the false sage.

"Come, Wise Sir," said the king. "Let us go to the park and look into this odd matter."

So the king went out to his park, and the false sage went with him. He was sure now, from the bowmen's news, that the monkeys had all fled.

"That is just as good as if they were dead," he said in his own mind. "I shall be safe now."

The king went in at the park gate, with the false sage at his side. The monkey-king still sat on the arch above them.

As they went under the arch, the monkey-king hung down from it by one hand. With the other hand he could just reach the top of the false sage's head. Whisk! Off came the false top-knot.

The false sage put his hands to his head. He gave a start and a cry that made the king turn to look at him. He saw the false sage with no top-knot, and over him the monkey-king with the false top-knot in his hand.

"Why," cried the king, "you are not a Wise Sir at all!"

"No, Sire," said the false sage.

"Then," said the king, "monkey fat is *not* a cure for elephant burns?"

"No, Sire," said the false sage again.

"I can keep you no longer as my Wise Sir if you are not one," said the king.

"No, Sire," said the false sage yet again.

So the king sent the false sage away. And the monkey-king went to the jungle to bring his monkeys back to the king's park.

From then on, the king made much of the monkeys in his park.

"For," he said, "I did not know a false sage from a true one. But my monkeys did!"

# The Lotus Garland

A son was once born to a king of one of the lands in India. A sage who read the stars came to the king and said, "Sire, I have read in the stars that the son of this son just born to you will be king of all India, and that he will not take the other lands in war, but they will all fall to him in peace."

When this came to the ears of the other kings, they sent messengers to say: "Let the son just born to you be left in the forest, that the wild beasts may eat him. We will not let him grow up to have a son who will take all our lands from us."

The king sent his reply: "The stars do not say that the son of my son will take your lands from you. They say that your lands will all fall to him in peace."

And the other kings answered: "We will not risk it. Let your son be left in the forest, or we will all come and take your city and kill you as well as your son."

Then the king said to his queen, "Our son will not be safe if we keep him here. It will be best to send him into the forest, as the other kings bid us do. But not for the wild beasts to eat. We will send him to a hermit to be raised as a sage, not a king. And I will take a vow that he shall never be king in my place."

"My lord," said the queen, "why not send the Five Marks of a King with him? Then, if ever a son *is* born to our son, he can send the child back to us with the

Marks, and we shall know from them who he is."

"Lady dear, that is well said," replied the king.

So the king sent his son to a hermit in the forest to be raised; and with him the Five Marks of a King — a sword of gold, a diadem of gems, a fan of peacock feathers, slippers of straw, and a white silk umbrella.

"If a son is ever born to my son," the king told the hermit, "send the child back to me with these Five Marks of a King."

Not long after this, a child was born to the king of the land to the north. This child was a girl. And the sage who read the stars came to this king and said, "Sire, I have read in the stars that the son of the child just born to you will be king of all India, and that he will not take the other lands in war, but they will all fall to him in peace."

When this came to the ears of the other kings, they sent messengers to say: "Let the child just born to you be left in the forest, that the wild beasts may eat her. We will not let her grow up to have a son who will take all our lands from us."

The king sent back to tell them: "The stars do not say that the son of my child will take your lands from you. They say that your lands will all fall to him in peace."

But the other kings replied: "We will not risk it. Let your child be left in the forest, or we will all come and take your city and kill you as well as her."

Then the king said to his queen, "Our child will not be safe if we keep her here. It will be best to send her into the forest, as the other kings bid us do. But not for the wild beasts to eat. We will send her to a hermit to be raised. And I will take a vow that she shall never take her place as a princess or a queen."

"My lord," said his queen, "let me go with her. No hermit can take such care of a girl as her own mother can."

"Lady dear, that is well said," replied the king.

So the king sent his child to a hermit in the forest to be raised; and with her went the queen.

Now the forest lay in the south of that land and stretched into the north of the land next to it. A river cut the two lands off from each other.

On the south bank of this river, a hermit took care of the little prince. And on the north bank of this same river, a way off, the other hermit and the queen took care of the little princess.

But on both sides of the river the forest was so thick that years went by and still the prince and the princess had not seen each other.

Now on the north bank of the river, just by the queen's hut, grew a mango tree. It bent over the river, and the princess often sat in it, even when she had grown up.

One day she had been into the river to pick lotus buds. She went and sat in her mango tree while she wove the lotus buds into a garland. She set the garland on her head, and bent to look at her face in the water.

The garland fell from her head, and the river swept it swiftly out of her reach.

Now some way down the river, the prince went in to bathe. As he rose and fell with the water, he saw a lotus garland float by. He swam to it, and took it in his hand. To it clung three long, jet-black hairs, as fine as silk.

"A girl has worn this garland," said the prince, "a girl with long, jet-black hair as fine as silk. And not long ago, for the lotus buds are still fresh. Can a girl live here in the forest? I must go and find her!"

And he began to swim up the river. He had swum a long way when at last a sweet song blew to him out of a mango tree that stood on the far bank.

As he drew near, he saw that a girl sat in the tree. She had long, jet-black hair, as fine as silk, like the three hairs on the lotus garland. And as soon as he saw her, he fell in love with her.

"Lady, is this lotus garland yours?" he asked. And he held it up out of the water.

"It is, Sir," she said and she bent down to take it.

He swam right under the mango tree and gave her back her garland.

"Lady," he said, "are you a girl or a fairy?"

"I am a girl of flesh and blood, Sir," she told him. "Are you flesh and blood too? Or are you a water-man?"

"I, too, am flesh and blood," he said. "I am a prince, a prince of the land on the far side of the river. But I have to live in the forest, for the stars say my son will be king of all the lands in India."

"So do the stars say *my* son will," she told him. "That is why *I* have to live in the forest. For I am a princess of the land on *this* side of the river."

"Do you think your son and my son can be the same?" asked the prince.

"Let us go and ask my mother," said the princess.

So the prince came up out of the river; and the princess came down out of the mango tree; and they went to the queen in her hut. And when the prince had told her who he was, she saw that they must marry each other.

She sent for the king, and he came in secret to the forest. The prince took him to his hermit; and as soon as the king saw the Five Marks of a King that the hermit kept for the prince's son, he, too, knew that these two must marry each other. So he gave the princess to the prince to be his wife.

When he went back to his city, he sent for the sage who had read the stars. He told the sage what had come to pass and asked him, "Wise Sir, why did it come to pass *this* way?"

And the sage told him, "Sire, the man who is to be King of all India will need to be so gentle and so wise that he has to grow up as a hermit, and even his father and mother have had to grow up in the care of hermits, too."

In time, the prince and princess had a son. He, too, grew up in the forest. And when he came of age, his father sent him back to his own father, with the Five Marks of a King. And his mother sent him, also, to *her* father. And both old kings were full of joy, and gave up both lands to him.

And he was so gentle, wise and good that his fame went far and wide, so that when kings of other surrounding lands died, the wise men of each land sent to him to beg him to be king.

And so it came to pass that in time he was king of all the lands in India, and yet, as the sage had read in the stars, he did not take them in war, but they all fell to him in peace.

# The Boy Who Found Water

There was once a sand-pilot whose job was to take caravans of ox-carts safely across the Great Desert.

In the Great Desert, the sand went on and on and on. It took a week to cross. It had no tracks and no trees. The only grass grew in small, thin patches near each spring. And in the Great Desert, the springs were few and far between.

So the men with the ox-carts had to take wood and water with them into the Great Desert, as well as food to last them for a week.

One night, the sand-pilot set out with a caravan of ox-carts to cross the Great Desert. His small son went with him.

They had to go by night, for by day the sand was too hot for man or ox to step on. The sand-pilot told the way to go from the stars.

He lay on his back on the top of the first ox-cart, with his eyes on the night sky. The ox-carts went in a long file, and a rope passed from the heads of the oxen that drew each cart to the back of the cart in front of it. So when the sand-pilot bore to the left, all the file of ox-carts in turn bore to the left. When he bore to the right, so did they.

And so the caravan went on all night, led by the stars. As soon as it grew light, the men put the ox-carts in a ring. They laid a cloth roof from cart to cart, to make a big tent to keep out the sun.

They freed the oxen from the yokes and fed them. They took oil and rice and wood and water out of the carts, and they lit a fire to cook a meal.

After the meal, they lay all day in the shade of the big tent-roof, and slept till the heat of the day was over.

When the sun went down, the sand grew cool. Then the men ate again, yoked the oxen to the carts again, and went on all night again, still led by the stars.

For six days and nights they did this. Then the sand-pilot said, "This will be our last day in the Great Desert. One more night led by the stars, then we shall pass into a land of grass and trees again."

So the men made the camp for the last time. They lay and slept all day in the shade of the tent-roof. At dusk, they ate the last meal, then they threw away the wood that was still left in the carts; for once they were out of the Great Desert, they had no more need of it.

Then the ox-carts set out. In the first one, the sand-pilot lay on his back to steer them by the stars. His small son lay at his side.

Plod, plod went the oxen. Jog, jog went the cart. For six nights the sand-pilot had had no sleep. But now the swing and sway of the ox-cart began to lull him, and he slid into a deep sleep.

In his sleep, he drew the left rein tight. So his oxen went to the left. And all the long file of ox-carts went to the left after them.

The left rein was still tight, so the oxen still went to the left. All night they went to the left, so that they made a big half-ring across the sand.

The sand-pilot's small son lay and slept, too, at his father's side. When he woke, he lay on his back to look at the sky. He was to be a sand-pilot, too, when he grew up, so he knew a little about the map the stars made on the sky at night. And now that map did not look quite right to him.

"Father," he said, "what is wrong with the stars?"

But his father only gave a snore. Then the boy knew that his father slept. He shook him, to wake him up.

"Father!" he cried. "Wake up! The sky is all back to front!"

The sand-pilot woke with a start. One look at the stars, and he saw that what his small son said was true. He drew up his oxen with a jerk.

"Halt!" he cried to the man on the next ox-cart. "Pass back the word to stop all the carts. We have lost our way!"

The man on each cart cried the news to the next. The long file of ox-carts came to a halt. And just then the sun came up. They saw in the sand the marks still left by the camp they had left last night.

"See, we are back at our last camp!" they cried.

"We must camp here again till nightfall," said the sand-pilot.

"But how can we cook a meal?" cried the rest of the men. "We have no water, and we threw away what was left of our wood."

"Even so, we must spend the day here," said the sand-pilot. "It is too hot to go on by day, and I do not know the way till the stars come out."

So the men freed the oxen from the yokes. They put the carts in a ring. They set up the tent-roof. And each lay down by his own cart, and hid his head miserably in his robe.

But the sand-pilot's small son was not able to rest. He got up, and went to his father and said, "Father, let me look in the sand round the camp while it is still cool. I may find some of the wood we threw away."

"The wood is no good if we have no water, my son," said the sand-pilot. "Still, go and look if you wish. But do not get lost. Do not go out of sight of the camp."

So the boy went to and fro across the sand. He found some bits of the wood. He took them back to the camp, then went out again to look for more. He found more, and took that back too.

Then the sand-pilot said, "Do not go out again, my son. The sun and the sand grow too hot."

"Just this last time, Father," replied the boy. And he went out this time on the far side of the camp.

This time he saw a splash of green on the skyline. He went to see what it was, and found that it was a small, thin patch of grass.

"A spring must be near here," he said. "In the Great Desert, grass will only grow near water. How is it that my father did not know about this spring?"

He went to and fro to look for the spring. But he did not find one.

"Then the water must be *under* the grass," he said.

He ran back in the hot sun to the camp.

"Father! Father! I have found grass!" he cried.

At this, all the men sprang up and came in a crowd to meet him.

"Did you find the spring?" they cried.

"No," he said. "The water must be down below."

"Then let us dig down to it," all the men cried.

Each took a spade from his ox-cart. They went with the boy to his patch of grass, and they all began to dig.

It was hot in the sun. But still the men dug. They dug down and down in the hot sand under the patch of grass. At last a spade rang on rock.

Still they dug till they laid the rock bare. It was long; it was wide. If water slept below, this shelf of rock cut them off from it.

"So near, and yet so far!" cried the men. "What good to go on? How can we dig up a bed of rock?"

And back they went to the camp, each bent to his spade as an old man bends to his staff. They lay down in the shade of the tent-roof in despair.

But the boy did not go with them. He crept down to the bed of rock. He lay flat on it. He put his ear to it and thought, "I am sure I can hear water!"

Then he saw a line that ran along the face of the rock.

"That will be its weak spot," said the boy. "If the rock will crack at all, it will be along this rift."

He took up his spade, and stuck its edge into the rift to act as a wedge. Then he ran back in the noonday heat to the camp.

The ox-carts had a sledgehammer to drive in pegs when the tent-roof was put up. The boy found the sledgehammer. Back to the rock he went with it, and struck a hard blow at the spade that was his wedge.

The rock split along the cleft. Out of that split, a jet of water shot up, as tall as a palm tree.

At the boy's shout, his father got up to look. He told the rest of the men. Out of the camp they all ran, full of joy, to drink and to bathe.

Then back to the camp they went, light of heart and light of step. They lit a fire with the wood the boy had found. They took water from the new spring to cook rice. They ate. They gave the oxen food and water. They gave thanks.

They set up a flag to mark the new spring. And at nightfall they set out again. This time the sand-pilot did not sleep, but kept his eyes on the stars. And at dawn they came out of the Great Desert into a land of grass and trees.

The boy grew up to be a sand-pilot, like his father. And each time he led a caravan across the Great Desert, and the ox-carts stood in a ring by the spring, the men said, "Tell us how you found this spring, O Boy Who Found Water."

For all his life, even when he grew old, he kept the name of the Boy Who Found Water.

# The Speech of Beasts

Long, long ago, all men were able to speak with the birds and the beasts. Then, as time went by, the speech of the birds and the beasts grew less and less clear to men.

At last the time came when only wise men understood what the birds and beasts said when they spoke. The wise men knew a spell that made this speech clear. They could pass on this spell to other men, but they had to be good men, and in need of the help this spell gave them.

One day, a king's sage died. The king was left in need of a new sage to help him to rule his land well. He said to his men, "Go out and seek a wise man to take the place of my sage who has died."

So the king's men went out into all parts of the land to seek a wise man. One by one they came back to the king. But not one of them had found him a sage. At last the last one of all came back.

"Sire," he said, "up in the hills I found a hermit who is very wise. So strong is his goodwill that all the birds and beasts of that part live in peace with each other. He is just the sage you need. But he will not come."

"Then *I* will go to him," said the king, "and beg him to come."

So the king went up to the hills. He found the hermit at the door of his hut. Birds and beasts gathered round him in flocks.

"Wise Sir," said the king, "my sage has died. I need a new sage to help me to rule my land well. I have come to beg you to do this."

But the hermit said, "Sire, that is a good task for a sage. But my task lies here in the hills."

"What is your task?" asked the king.

"I think goodwill to all things," said the hermit. "And this way the birds and beasts of this part live in peace with each other. But I see a way to help you. For if the speech of birds and beasts is clear to you, you will in time grow so wise that you will need no sage."

"What must I do for it to grow clear to me?" asked the king.

And the hermit told him, "I can teach you a spell that will make it so."

"Teach me, Wise Sir," said the king.

"First I must tell you," said the hermit, "that only a wise man may pass on this spell; and then only to a good man; and then only if he is in need of the help this spell will give him. You must pass the spell on to no-one. If you do, you will die that same day."

"I will not pass it on, Wise Sir," said the king.

So the hermit told him the spell.

"Say it at the first meal you eat when you get back to your palace," he said.

So the king left the hermit with his flocks of birds and beasts. He went down from the hills to the plain, and came again to his own city.

When the king arrived back at his palace, he sat down to eat with the queen. As he ate, he shut his eyes, and said the spell in his own mind.

The queen asked, "Lord, why do you shut your eyes?"

"Lady dear, that is my secret," answered the king. As he spoke, he took a sweetmeat out of the golden dish. He bit into it, and a crumb of it fell to the floor.

At once an ant ran to the crumb and cried out, "Ants! Ants! The king has upset his honey cart! Come quick, and eat honey!"

At this, the king put his hands to his sides, and shook with mirth.

"My Lord, why are you so merry?" asked the queen.

"Lady dear, that is my secret," said the king.

After the meal, the queen went to her bath. When she came back, her skin smelled sweet with the oils her slave girls had spread on it.

A fly said, "Wife, it is time we went to bed."

"Not yet, my love," said the fly's wife. "The queen has just come from her bath. She smells so sweet, let us stand on her nose and sniff."

And both flies flew to the queen and stood on her nose, and began to wave their legs in joy.

At this, the king again put his hands on his hips, and shook with mirth.

"My Lord, why are you so merry?" asked the queen again.

And again the king told her, "Lady dear, that is my secret."

"That is the third time you have told me that," said the queen. "Tell me this secret, my Lord."

And she gave him no peace till he told her what the ant and the flies had said.

"How did you know this, my Lord?" she asked then. "How can I be sure you did not make this up, to hide the true secret from me?"

"I did not make it up," said the king. "The hermit in the hills told me a spell that has made the speech of birds and beasts clear to me."

"Tell me that spell!" cried the queen.

"It must not be told," said the king.

"Tell it me! Tell it me!" she cried, again and again.

At last the king said, "If I do tell anyone, I must die."

"Even if you must die, tell it to me!" cried the queen.

And she gave him no peace till at last the king said, worn out, "Very well, Lady dear. I will tell it to you."

"When will you tell it to me?" asked the queen. "Tell it to me now!"

But the king said, "The hermit told me this spell to help me to grow wise. It will be a pity to get no good from it before I die. I will first hear the speech of beasts a third time, and see if it brings me wisdom. Then I will tell you the spell, since you force me to."

"Go out and hear it now, dear Lord," cried the queen. "It is hard for me to wait to hear it, too."

The king rose, and went out of his palace to his park.

He went to his stone bench and sat down. This bench stood under a big fig tree.

In this fig tree two monkeys sat and ate figs. One took only ripe figs. The other took them as they came to his hand. He bit them, and if they were still green, he threw them down.

"How silly you are," said the first monkey, "to waste our figs so! The green figs will grow big and ripe if they are left."

"I may be silly," said the second monkey, "but I am not so silly as the king."

"Why so?" asked the first monkey.

"Well, is he not silly," asked the second, "to die at the whim of a wife who cares more for his secret than for his life?"

"Monkey, that is true!" cried the king. "Now I see why the hermit said, *If the speech of birds and beasts is clear to you, you will grow wise.*"

"You grow wise too late, O King," said the second monkey.

"Yes," said the king, "for I have promised to tell her the spell; and so I must."

Then the first monkey said, "But can you not also tell her that he who hears the spell must first have sixty lashes of the whip?"

Now the king put his hands on his hips and shook with mirth.

"I can. And I will," he cried. He left the park and went back to the palace, and as he arrived he sent for a slave with a whip. The queen ran to meet him.

"Did you hear the speech of beasts a third time, dear lord?" she asked.

"I did," said the king.

"And did it bring you wisdom, dear Lord?" asked the queen.

"It did," said the king.

"Then tell me the spell now, dear Lord," said the queen.

"I had quite forgotten to tell you, Lady dear," said the king, "that anyone who is to be told this spell must first have sixty lashes of the whip." And he beckoned to the slave with the whip who stood by. The slave raised the whip and cracked the lash two or three times, then came towards the queen.

"Then, Lord, do keep your secret spell, and tell the slave to stop!" cried the queen.

The king did so. The queen did not ask for the spell

again as long as she lived. And, just as the hermit had said, in time the speech of birds and beasts made the king grow so wise that he had no need of a sage to help him to rule the land well.

# Prince Grit-in-the-Eye

A king once had a son who was so selfish that men said of him, "He is like a thorn in the hand; he is like sand in a dish of rice; he is like grit in the eye."

And so he got the name of Prince Grit-in-the-Eye.

One day he went to fish in the river. A storm came on, and it grew as black as night. Prince Grit-in-the-Eye flew into a rage, and began to rain blows on all his men as if they were to blame.

One said to the next, "If he is as bad as this as a prince, what will he do to us when he is king?"

"Best to get rid of him here and now," said the other. "In you go, you pest!"

And they flung him straight into the river.

When they returned to the king, he asked why his son was not with them.

"Is he not here yet, Sire?" they cried. "It grew so dark, we lost each other in the storm."

The king sent them back to the river to seek the prince. But they found no trace of him.

He had been swept along in the storm till the strong current threw him on to one end of a tree trunk that floated down the river. He clung fast to this in the dark, while uttering cries of fear.

A hiss came in his ear: "No-one will hear you, Prince Grit-in-the-Eye. No-one lives near the river just here."

"Who spoke?" cried Prince Grit-in-the-Eye.

The hiss came again in the dark: "I am a snake. The storm swept me out of my home in the bank of the river. With me is a rat, who was swept away too."

As it grew less dark, the prince saw the snake and the rat at the other end of his tree trunk. And still the strong tide swept them on.

At a bend in the river, the flood tore up a tree by its roots. It fell with a huge splash that made the tree trunk rock. A parrot flew out of the tree; but the rain beat her down. She landed on the tree trunk and clung with her claws, the prince on one side of her, the snake and rat on the other.

"Shout for help when I do," said the parrot. "Just by the next bend lives a hermit."

The prince cried with a snort, "What good is that? How can one man save me from such a flood as this?"

"He is as strong as an elephant," said the parrot. "He will save us all. We are near the bend; shout now!"

She began to cry out in a loud, shrill squawk, "Help! Help!"

So the prince, too, began to shout, "Help! Help!"

The hermit ran out of his hut and down the bank to the edge of the water. He saw the tree trunk, with its living cargo.

Into the water he sprang. He took hold of the log, and drew it to the bank with one long pull. He set the prince, the parrot, the snake and the rat safe on land. Then he led them all four to his hut.

He lit a fire. He set a stool at one side of it for the prince. He set down the snake and the rat and the parrot in front of it.

Then he gave them all food. Prince Grit-in-the-Eye shook with rage, for the hermit fed the snake and the rat and the parrot first, and left him till last.

"Why do you feed me last?" he cried. "I am a man,

while they are only beasts. I am a prince, and they are less than the dust under my feet."

"You are strong; they are weak," replied the hermit.

After some days, the river went down, and the prince, the snake, the rat and the parrot all went home.

As the snake left the hut, he said to the hermit, "Holy Sir, I owe my life to you. By my home grow herbs that heal. If ever you have need of them, just call *Snake!* and I will come to you."

As the rat left the hut, he said to the hermit, "Holy Sir, I owe my life to you. I have sharp teeth. If ever you have need of them, just call *Rat!* and I will come to you."

As the parrot left the hut, she said to the hermit, "Holy Sir, I owe my life to you. By my home is a rice patch. If ever you need food, just call *Parrot!* and I will come to you."

As the prince left the hut, he said to the hermit, "Come to me, hermit, when I am king, and you will see what I will give you."

Not long after this, the king died, and Prince Grit-in-the-Eye was king in his place. If he had been bad as a prince, he was twice as bad as a king.

All over the city a wail went up: "He grinds us down like sugarcane in a sugarmill. Oh, *why* did the hermit save him?"

One day, the hermit had to go to the city to get salt. As King Grit-in-the-Eye went through the streets in procession, he saw the yellow robe of a sage. He bent to look, and he saw it was the hermit.

He was reminded of how the hermit had fed him

last. He grew hot with rage.

"Did I not say to you, hermit," he cried, "*Come to me when I am king, and you will see what I will give you?*"

"You did, Sire," said the hermit.

"Take this hermit and flog the skin off his back. Then bind him hand and foot, and cast him into a deep pit. Let him have no food or drink. Let him lie in the pit till he dies," said King Grit-in-the-Eye to his men.

The king's men took the hermit, and did all that the king had told them. Then they cast him into a deep pit and left him to die.

When all was still, the hermit cried out, "Rat!" as he lay in the pit. And into the pit ran the rat.

"What can I do for you, Holy Sir?" asked the rat.

"Can you free me from my bonds?" asked the hermit.

"I can, Holy Sir," said the rat. "Lie still, and I will bite."

And the rat bit at the tight bonds until they split and the hermit was free of them.

Then the hermit cried out, "Snake!" And into the pit slid the snake.

"What can I do for you, Holy Sir?" asked the snake.

"Can you heal my back?" asked the hermit.

"I can, Holy Sir," said the snake. "Lie still, and I will lay my herbs on it."

And the snake laid his herbs on the hermit's raw back; and the pain left him, and new skin grew again.

Then the hermit cried out, "Parrot!" And into the pit flew the parrot.

"What can I do for you, Holy Sir?" asked the parrot.

"Can you bring me rice?" asked the hermit.

"I can, Holy Sir," said the parrot. "Lie still, and I will fetch it."

Soon parrot after parrot flew in a long flock to the pit. Each parrot held a grain of rice in her bill.

The king's men saw the parrots flying over the city.

"See, the sky is full of parrots!" they cried. "See, they fly to the pit where we cast the hermit!"

And they ran to the pit to find out why.

When they bent to look into the pit, they saw that in it sat the hermit, his hands and feet free of his bonds, new skin on his back, a heap of rice in front of him. A snake and a rat and a parrot were with him; and all the time more and more parrots flew in with more and more rice.

"This hermit must be a holy man," they cried. "Then why did the king make us punish him? And why did he wish him to die?"

Then the snake and the rat and the parrot all said, "We can tell you why." And they told them.

The king's men cried out with anger, and back to the city they ran and told everyone they met.

All the people of the city were full of rage at what the king had done to the hermit. When they saw the king approaching in his procession, they ran to meet him with loud shouts and with sticks and clubs held high.

When King Grit-in-the-Eye saw the angry crowd coming towards him, he shook with fear and ran as fast as he could out of the city gates and never came back.

Now King Grit-in-the-Eye had no son. So when they saw that he had gone for good, the people of the city all cried, "Who shall be king in his place? Let us make the hermit our king!"

So they took the hermit out of the pit, and they made him the king of the land. He took the snake and the rat and the parrot to live with him in his palace. And he was every bit as good a king as King Grit-in-the-Eye had been a bad one.

# Rats at the Lute

The Land of Kasi was the chief land in India. The king of Kasi was the chief king in India. And the king of Kasi's lute player was the best lute player in India. His name was Guttila.

One day, men from the Land of Kasi went to the next land with goods to sell. While they were there, a feast was held in the city.

As they sat at the feast, each with a garland on his head, they said, "Let us send for a lute player to play for us."

So they sent for a lute player, and one came. His name was Musila.

He tightened his lute strings, and began to play. When he came to the end of the air, he said in his own mind, "How well I play! How these men from Kasi will cheer and snap their fingers, and clap their hands!"

But not one cheer did the men of Kasi give; not one finger did they snap; not one hand did they clap.

"Did I play too sharp for them?" asked Musila in his own mind.

So for the next air he let down the strings a little. But still the men of Kasi sat glum at the feast.

So for his last air Musila made his strings quite slack. But still the men of Kasi sat glum at the feast.

Then Musila said to them, "Sirs, when I play my lute, why do I give you no joy?"

"Why, when did you play it?" they asked.

"Did you not hear it?" Musila asked in turn.

"We did," they said. "But were you not just tuning it?"

This made Musila roar with rage, "Sirs, I am the best lute player in all this land!"

"That well may be," said the men of Kasi. "But in Kasi we have the best lute player in all the world. Guttila's lute-tone is so sweet that beside it yours is as if you were rubbing a rush mat."

Then Musila flung down the gold they had paid him.

"Take back your fee," he cried. "But when you go back to Kasi, I will go with you."

So when the men of Kasi went back, Musila went with them. When they came to the king's city, Musila said to them, "Take me to this Guttila's house."

So they took him to Guttila's house, and left him at the door.

The door stood open, so Musila went in. He saw a lute hanging up on the wall. He took it down and began to play it.

Guttila's old blind mother sat at the far end of the room.

"Shoo, shoo!" she cried. "The rats are at that lute again. Rats, do not snap my son's lute strings. Shoo, shoo! Go away, you rats!"

Musila hung up the lute again, and did not say a word. But his face was grim.

Then Guttila came in. Musila said to him, "Sir, I have left my own land to beg you to teach me your art."

Guttila saw from his face that Musila was not a good man, and he did not wish to teach him. But Musila gave him no rest. So at last Guttila gave in.

"Teach me all you know," said Musila.

"I will," said Guttila.

It took a long time for Guttila to teach Musila all he knew. But at last Guttila said, "Musila, I have now told you all I know of my art. It is time for you to go back to your own land."

But Musila said to himself, "I will not go back to my own land. This city is the chief city in all India. Its king is the chief king. The best lute player in all the world has told me all he knows. I will stay and drive him out, and take his place."

So to Guttila he said, "Not so. I wish to wait upon the king."

"Very well," said Guttila. "I will tell the king."

So Guttila went to the king, and told him, "Sire, it is the wish of Musila the lute player to wait on you."

"Then let him do so," said the king. "His fee shall be half as much as your own."

When Guttila told this to Musila, Musila replied, "I will wait on the king only for the same fee as yours."

"Why so?" asked Guttila.

"Do I not know all that you know?" asked Musila.

"Yes, you do," said Guttila.

"Then the same fee is my due," said Musila.

"I will tell the king," said Guttila.

So Guttila told the king. "Yes, Guttila, he *may* know all that you know," replied the king, "but can he *play* as you play? You shall both play, and I will see. If *he* can play as well as you play, then I will pay him the same as you."

"When will you hold this test of lute-skill, Sire?" asked Guttila.

"In seven days time," answered the king.

And he sent his men to beat drums in the city, and to tell the news that a test of lute-skill was to be held at the king's gate in seven days time.

Guttila went out of the city to the king's park. To and fro, to and fro he went, till he wore a bare patch in the grass. He said as he went to and fro, "This test of lute-skill is a sad thing. If *I* am best, I win shame in that I did not teach Musila well. If *he* is best, I win shame as a lute player; and can I then keep my post with the king? But if I do *not* keep that post, how shall I then take care of my blind old mother?"

Now Sakka, the King of the Sky, sat on his throne in the air. And as Guttila went to and fro so sadly, Sakka bent to look down to find out why. And he saw Guttila go to and fro, to and fro on his bare patch of grass.

"Shame on Musila," said Sakka, "to make such a good man so sad. Musila will never play as well as Guttila. For Guttila is a good man, and he plies his art for love of it. But Musila is a bad man, and plies his art for greed. I see I must take a hand in his."

So Sakka sent a rat into Guttila's house to snap one of his lute strings.

The rat ran up to the lute. *Snap* went the lute string.

"Shoo, shoo!" cried the blind old mother. "Go away, rats! Do not snap my son's lute strings! Shoo, shoo!"

When Guttila came in, she said, "Look at your lute, my son. A rat has been at it again, and has snapped a string."

"I will put a new string in," said Guttila. He took down the lute, and began idly to play it before putting in the new string.

"Why, my son," cried his mother, "you play as well with only six strings as with seven!"

Next day, Sakka sent two rats, and two strings went *snap*. And Guttila found he was able to play as well with five strings as with seven.

The next day Sakka sent three rats; and the next day four; the next, five; the next, six. The last day before the trial of lute-skill he sent seven, and all seven strings went *snap*.

And even then Guttila was able to play as well as ever, on the bare lute, with no strings at all.

"Have no fear; you will win the trial of lute-skill, my son, with this new gift," said his blind old mother.

The next day was the day of the trial of lute-skill. Guttila put seven new strings on his lute. He bent over his blind old mother, for her to kiss his head and wish him well. Then out he went with his lute to the king's gate.

At the king's gate, a rich tent of silk had been put up, with flags all over it and with fresh lotus buds all over its floor. Under it stood the king's seat.

On all four sides of the palace courtyard, rows of seats had been set up, tier above tier. All the seats were full. All the men of Kasi had come to hear the test of lute-skill.

Guttila sat in his place in the midst of the courtyard. Musila sat in *his* place, face to face with him. Each began to tune his lute. Then the king threw down a garland, and the test of lute-skill began.

Guttila and Musila, each in turn, played the same air on his lute. The lute tone of both was so sweet that the crowd broke into cries of joy.

Then Guttila broke his B-string. From its tips it still sent out sweet tones.

At this, Musila broke *his* B-string. But the string *he* broke was mute and left gaps in his music.

Then Guttila broke the next string, then the next, then the next, then the next, till only the bare lute was left. Yet even then, Guttila's sweet music still played out over all the city.

But when Musila did the same, his music was so bad that the king put his hands over his ears. And all the men of Kasi did as the king did.

"Guttila wins! Guttila wins the trial of lute-skill!" cried the crowd.

The king threw down a second garland, and gave a nod. And a child took a third garland from the king's hand, and ran to set it on Guttila's head.

Then Musila sprang to his feet, and flung down his lute.

He cried to the king, "Sire, this test was not a just test. Guttila has lied to me."

"How so?" asked the king.

"He said he had told me all he knew," cried Musila. "But he did not show me how to snap the lute strings and still play as well as ever."

"Is this true, Guttila?" asked the king.

"It is true that I did not teach Musila how to do this," said Guttila. "And yet I told him no lies, and I *did* teach him all I knew. For it is only in this last week that this new skill has come to me."

And he told the king all about the seven rats.

"I see the hand of Sakka in this," said the king. "For Sakka gives more and more skill to the man who plies his art in love; but to the man who plies it in greed he gives no help. Musila, I think the time has come for you to go back to your own land."

"Yes, Musila," cried the crowd. "Go back to your own land!"

And they shouted at him till he went away. So Musila was glad to go back to his own land. And Guttila kept his post as the king's chief lute player, and was still the best lute player in all the world, and loved by all the people for being such a good man.

# Prince Sun and Princess Moon

There was once a princess who was so lovely that it was said of her: "When she stands at her window at full moon, it is as if two moons came up."

And this is how she got her name of Princess Moon.

When she grew up, the king her father said to her, "My child, it is time for you to marry. But I fear we shall never find a prince fit to marry my Princess Moon."

"My father," said Princess Moon, "find me a prince keen of eye, quick of mind, strong of arm, wise of heart and loved by the gods; and I will marry him and love him till I die."

Then the king drew up five tests to find out if a man was keen of eye, quick of mind, strong of arm, wise of heart, and loved by the gods. And he sent news of the tests into all the surrounding lands.

Princes from many kingdoms came to try to pass the tests. But all the princes went away again, for not one of them was able to pass the five tests.

At last a prince came; and as soon as the princess saw him from her window, she fell in love with him. For when he stood, he was like a flame of fire. And when he sat, he was like an image of fine gold.

His name was Prince Sun.

Then Princess Moon cried out to all her gods, "Let Prince Sun pass all the tests. For if I do not marry him,

I feel as if I shall die. But if I do marry him, I feel as if I shall live for ever!"

The day came for Prince Sun's first test. This was to find out if he was keen of eye. The king led him along a path in his park till they came to two snakes that lay sleeping in the sun.

"Are they king-snakes or queen-snakes?" asked the king.

Prince Sun let his eyes go over them from top to tail. Then he said, "The one to the right is a king-snake. The one to the left is a queen."

"How can you tell?" asked the king.

And Prince Sun told him, "His tail is thick; hers is thin. His head is round; hers is oval. His eyes are big; hers are small. He is long; she is short."

"You pass the first test, Prince Sun," said the king.

The news ran all round the city. And all the city was glad for the sake of Princess Moon.

The day came for Prince Sun's second test. This was to find out if he was quick of mind. The king led Prince Sun out into the courtyard of his palace. He gave him a bag of rice.

"You are to cook me this rice," he said, "in no pot, and with no water. You must burn no wood. You must send the rice to me in a bowl held by two hands, but by no man or woman. I shall stand at my window on the upper floor; the rice must not be sent up any steps to reach me, and it must not come to me along the ground, nor yet by air or by water."

A crowd stood round Prince Sun to see him try to pass this test. He said to the man next him, "Bring me a clay bowl, for that is not a pot. And fill it with snow, for that is not water."

He put the rice in the snow in the clay bowl. Then he said, "Bring me straw to burn in place of wood."

He set his rice to cook on his fire of straw. When the rice was soft, he sent for a fresh bowl, and put it into this.

Then he said to a child who stood near, "Take this bowl to the king; you are not yet man or woman."

He put back his head to look up at the king's window, and saw that the high wall around the courtyard came to an end beside it.

So he set the child on the wall; and the child ran along the top of the wall to the king's window; and the king took the bowl of rice.

"You pass the second test, Prince Sun," said the king.

A roar of joy went up from the crowd; and again the news ran like wildfire round the city. And all the city was glad for the sake of Princess Moon.

The day came for Prince Sun's third test. This was to find out if he was wise of heart.

Now the king's seat was set up in the king's gateway, as it was when he sat to judge any case or to right any wrong. It was his custom then to take off his straw slippers, and to put them on the seat beside him.

When he spoke to judge a case, the slippers beat on each other if he was wrong; if he was right, they lay still.

So now the king put Prince Sun in his seat to judge a case; and he took off his straw slippers, and put them at Prince Sun's side.

The case Prince Sun had to judge was that of two women, who both said a baby was hers.

Prince Sun sent for the two women and the baby. He drew a line on the ground, and laid the baby across it.

To one of the women he said, "Take the child by his hands."

To the other he said, "Take the child by his feet."

They did as he told them. Then he said, "Now pull."

Again they did as he told them. The baby gave a little cry of pain; and at once the woman who held his hands let go, and stood and wept. But the other held fast to the child.

Then Prince Sun said, "She who stands and weeps is the mother."

All eyes were on the slippers at his side. The slippers lay still.

"How did you tell?" asked the king.

And Prince Sun asked him back, "Who will feel most tender towards the child, the mother or not the mother?"

"The mother," replied the king.

"Then is she who held fast to the child when it cried out in pain most tender?" asked Prince Sun. "Or she who let go?"

"She who let go," answered the king.

And to the mother he said, "Mother, take your child."

The mother bent, and took the child that the other woman had now put down again. As she held him in her arms, she cried, "Live long and happy, O King! Live long and happy, Prince Sun!"

And all the crowd took up the cry: "Live long and happy, Prince Sun! Live long and happy with our Princess Moon!"

But Prince Sun had first to pass a fourth test. He had to show that he was strong of arm.

News was sent into all the streets of the city that in seven days Prince Sun was to wrestle with the best wrestler in all the land. To pass the test, Prince Sun must throw this wrestler, yet he must not lay a hand on him.

A ring for the match was set up in front of the king's gate. All the city was in a whirl. Row after row of seats were filled: tier above tier above tier.

The prize wrestler came to the match along the Street of the Washer-Men. As he came, he stole bright robes. Clad in them, he went down into the ring, a garland on his head, earrings in his ears.

He began to strut to and fro, to jump, to shout, to clap his hands at the crowd.

Then Prince Sun came into the ring. He wore only a gold undercloth. In his hands he held a thick elephant strap. As he went past the elephant stables, he had bent to pick it up.

The crowd sent up a cheer of joy and goodwill at the sight of him.

"But how *can* he win, if he may not lay a hand on our man?" they asked. "It will be sad if our man wins. Prince Sun is just the right prince for our Princess Moon."

Then the match began. The prize wrestler bore down on Prince Sun like a huge ape, his hands stretched out to take him and grip him fast.

But Prince Sun flung out one end of the strap he held. It wrapped round the wrestler and shot back to the prince. He held both ends in one hand; and with that one hand he caught the wrestler in the loop of the strap, swung him round his head, and flung him to the ground.

The wrestler lay still in the dust. The crowd cried out to him to rise up and go on with the match. But he shook his head with a groan.

So again the crowd cried out, as before, "Live long and happy, Prince Sun! Live long and happy with our Princess Moon!"

But Prince Sun had still one more test to pass. It was the test to show if he was loved by the gods.

All the city asked, "What test can the king find that will show this?"

And the king told Prince Sun, "Make me a park in one night, with a lake to match it, and with a palace to match them both."

"But, Sire," cried Prince Sun, "no man can do such a thing!"

"That is true," said the king. "But if the gods love him, and wish him to marry Princess Moon, they will do it for him."

That night, Prince Sun went to his room and lay on his bed to think. He did not feel it right to beg the gods to win this test for him; yet he knew he could not pass the test without help from them.

Now Sakka, the King of the Sky, sat on his throne of air. And as Prince Sun lay on his bed, with all this in his mind, Sakka bent down to look. He saw Prince Sun on his bed. He saw right into his mind.

So Sakka came down from the sky. He came dressed as a sage, in a yellow robe, with his hair done up in a top-knot; he went into Prince Sun's room.

"Prince, what are you worrying about?" he asked.

And Prince Sun told him, "Wise Sir, the king bids me make him a park, a lake and a palace, all in one night. That is what I am worrying about."

"Then think of it no more, Prince," Sakka said. "If the gods love you and wish you to marry Princess Moon, they will do it for you. Sleep now, my son, and see what the dawn will bring you."

Then Sakka, in his yellow robe and top-knot, went from the room. And Prince Sun lay down and slept peacefully.

At dawn, men came into the city in haste with news for the king.

"Sire," they said, "near our village, a new palace in a park has grown up in the night."

With joy the king went back with them.

As they drew near, he saw that all round the new park ran a high red wall, with a fine gate under a carved archway.

When he went into the park, he found it green and cool, with all kinds of rare trees and shrubs and plants. Grass and branches were bright with buds; the air was sweet; birds flew from tree to tree, and bees from bloom to bloom.

Then the king came to the lotus lake. Its water was like a gem, clear and full of light. The water was as blue as the sky, yet the light that came from it was as golden as the sun. Rings of lotus grew round its rim, blue and white and pink.

The king walked past the lake and came to the palace. It was like a palace in the sky.

Its walls were of clear glass, held up by posts of gold, set thick with gems. Along the clear glass walls hung nets of golden bells. Flags of gold and silver flew from its many bright gables; and golden birds sat on them and sang sweet songs.

And from the golden gate of the palace Princess Moon came out to meet him, a lotus garland in her hand.

"All is as you wish it to be, my child," said her father. "You shall marry your Prince Sun, and this palace shall be your home."

And so it was. And so it still is, if they both live.

# Big Sage and Little Sage

A village stood at the edge of the jungle. The small boys and girls from the village huts used to go into the jungle every day to play.

One day, a tiger sprang out at them, then sprang away with a child in his teeth.

After that, the grown-ups said to the small boys and girls, "You must never again go into the jungle to play."

"Then where *can* we play?" asked the small boys and girls.

"You must play in sight of the village," they were told.

"But tigers come as near as that, too," said the small boys and girls.

One of the boys was only seven years old. But even at that age he was so wise that he was known as Little Sage. His skin and eyes were not brown like the rest, but golden.

So now Little Sage said, in his high piping voice, "Then let us make a play hall of our own to play in. Then our mothers and fathers will know we are safe when we go out to play."

"That is a good plan," said the rest. "But how shall we get the things we need to make it with?"

"Let us each ask our father for a log to help to make the walls," said Little Sage. "And let us each ask our mother for twenty reeds to thatch the roof."

The boys and girls all did this. The mothers and

fathers were glad to help them with the things they needed. And soon the boys and girls of that village had a fine, safe hall to play in.

Now the king had a sage to help him rule the land. He was so tall and so fat that he was known as Big Sage.

When news of the play hall and how it came to be made reached the ears of the king, he said to Big Sage, "This boy is very wise for his years. Let us send for him."

But in his own mind Big Sage thought, "I must not let the king bring this child to court. If I do, one day he may drive me out and take my place; for in my heart I know that I am not a very wise man."

So to the king he said, "Sire, any child can be wise once in a way. Let us wait and see if he is wise again."

And the king let Big Sage have his way, and did not send at that time for Little Sage to come to his court.

Not long after this, a man in the next village spent all he had on two fine cows. As soon as he got them home, he put them in his grass patch, and sent his small son to tend them.

It was hot, and the boy soon went to sleep. A thief came by, and saw the boy fast asleep. So he took a stick, and drove off the two cows.

When the boy woke up, no cows were in the grass patch. He ran to and fro to look for them, and at last he found hoof marks in the mud. So he followed the track of the hoof marks, to try to catch the cows.

At last the hoof marks led him to the thief and the two cows.

"Sir," said the boy, "why do you drive away my
father's cows?"

"Your father's cows?" cried the thief. "These are *not*
your father's cows. These are *my* cows."

And still he drove them on.

The boy ran along at his side, and cried aloud that
the cows were his father's cows. And the thief cried
back that the cows were *his* cows.

In this way they came into Little Sage's village, and
a crowd ran to hear what the shouts were all about.
The crowd went along the track with them.

As they went past the play hall, Little Sage came to
the door to look out.

"Little Sage," cried the crowd, "here is a case for
you. Come out and judge it!"

So Little Sage came out to judge the case.

"What have you fed the cows on?" he asked the
thief.

"Bean flour and rice gruel," replied the thief.

"And what has your father fed them on?" Little Sage
asked the boy.

"How can a poor man like my father give his cows
bean flour and rice gruel?" cried the boy. "My father
has fed them on grass."

Then Little Sage said to the crowd, "Bring beans and
rice, and grind them up and mix them with water, and
give them to the cows."

They did this, and it made the cows sick.

Then Little Sage asked the crowd, "What did the
cows bring up when they were sick?"

And the crowd told him with a shout, "Grass, Little
Sage!"

At this, the thief took to his heels.

"We will see you safe home with your cows, boy,"
said some of the men.

And as the boy drove off his father's cows with the

men, he said to Little Sage, "May you live long, Little Sage, to help poor men!"

This, too, came to the ears of the king. He said to Big Sage, "You see, this little sage was right a second time. So shall we not send for him now?"

But Big Sage replied, "Sire, any village boy knows such things. You are city-bred, palace-bred; that is why you think it wise."

So again the king let Big Sage have his way, and did not send that time for Little Sage to come to him at his court.

One day not long after this, a girl from Little Sage's village sat among the cotton plants. And as she sat, she began to pluck at the tufts of cotton, and to spin a fine thread. Then she began to wind the thread until she had made it into a ball. But first she took up a mango seed that lay on the ground nearby, to make a firm core to wind it round.

As she went home, she passed a good spot to bathe in the river.

"It is hot. I will stop and bathe," she thought.

So she took off her dress and laid it on the grass. She left her cotton ball on the dress, and went down into the river.

As she came up the riverbank, she saw a girl go by. She saw the girl go back to her dress and take up the ball, then run on. So she put on her dress in haste, and ran to catch her up.

"Give me back my cotton ball," she said.

"*Your* ball?" cried the other. "It is *my* ball!"

And thus they still went on as they ran past the door

of the play hall, while a crowd ran from the huts to
hear what the shouts were all about.

Again Little Sage came to the door of the play hall
to look out.

"Come out, Little Sage," cried the crowd, "and judge
this case!"

So Little Sage came out to judge the case.

He asked the thief, "When you made this ball, what
did you wind it round?"

"A cotton seed," she said.

Then he asked the girl who had made it, "And what
did *you* wind it round?"

"A mango seed," she said.

Then Little Sage said to the crowd, "Look and see."

So they began to wind the long cotton thread into
a new ball. And when they came to the other end of
the thread, they found it was stuck fast to a mango
seed.

So Little Sage gave the cotton ball back to the girl
who had made it.

"May you live long, Little Sage, to help poor men!"
she cried.

This, too, came to the ears of the king. He said to Big
Sage, "Is it not time we sent for this small sage?"

"This sort of thing is not all that makes a sage,"
replied Big Sage. "Let us test him with other things
first."

So the king had a smooth pole sent to Little Sage.
It was the same size all along, from end to end. Little
Sage had to find out which end was the root-end, and
which the top.

"Bring it to the riverbank," said Little Sage.

The men of the village did so.

"Tie a string round it, halfway up," said Little
Sage.

The men of the village did so.

"Now hold fast to the end of the string, and let the pole down into the river," said Little Sage.

The men of the village did so.

The pole lay on the water. Then one end sank a little.

Then Little Sage asked the crowd, "Which is the light end, the root or the top?"

"The top, Little Sage," they cried.

"Then the end that sinks a little is the root," said Little Sage.

And he sent the pole back to the king, with a mark at each end to show which end was the root and which the top.

"Now we *will* send for him," said the king. And this time it was the king who had his way.

Little Sage had not been at court long when the queen had a gemstone fall from a bracelet she wore on her arm.

The thread it had hung from broke, and left a bit of itself in the long hole in the gem.

The king sent it to his gemsmiths for them to mend. They came to him, and said, "Sire, we have tried all the ways we can think of, but we have not been able to get the old thread out, nor to put the new one in."

Then the king said to Big Sage, "Can you tell them a way to do it?"

"Sire," said Big Sage, "this is not a matter for a sage. It is a matter of the gemsmith's craft."

Then the king asked Little Sage, "Can *you* do it, Little Sage?"

"I can try, Sire," said Little Sage. "I shall need a drop of honey and a thread of wool."

He put a smear of honey on the two ends of the hole in the gem, and a smear of it on the thread of wool. Then he put the end of the thread of wool a little way into the hole.

"And now," said Little Sage, "I shall need an anthill."

At this, Big Sage began to jeer, "What, you wish us to bring an anthill into the palace for you?"

"No, Wise Sir," said Little Sage. "An anthill need not come to *us*. *We* can go to the anthill."

So the king and his chief men went out to the king's park; and here they found an anthill. Little Sage put down the queen's gemstone on it. And they all stood round the anthill to see what happened next.

The smell of honey soon drew the ants to the gem. The long feelers of the ants, as fine as hairs, shot into the hole in the gem at its open end. They ate away the old thread with the honey on it. They bit hold of the end of the new thread, again with honey on it; they drew it out of the open end of the hole in the gem.

Then Little Sage took up the gem. It hung by the two ends of its new thread. He gave it to the queen.

And Big Sage said in his own mind, "If I fail in the next test, and this child again wins it, I shall not be able to stay with the king for very shame!"

That next test soon came. For one of the king's men told the king that he had seen a jewel in the lake in the king's park. The king went to look; and he, too, saw the jewel.

The king sent for Big Sage to come to the park.

When he came, he said to him, "Wise Sir, do you, too, see a jewel in this lake?"

"I see it, Sire," replied Big Sage.

"How shall we get it out?" asked the king.

"The best way," said Big Sage, "will be to send men to dive for it."

"Then do so," said the king.

And so Big Sage sent men into the lake to dive for the jewel. But not one of them found it.

"It looks to me, Sire," said Big Sage, "as if we shall have to drain out all the water, if we are ever to get the jewel."

"Then do so," said the king.

So the king sent for more of his men, and Big Sage had them drain out all the water from the lake. They got out all the mud; they even dug up the floor of the lake; but still no jewel was to be found.

"Fill the lake with water again," said the king. And when the men did so, the jewel was seen again, in just the same spot.

Then the king said to Little Sage, "Little Wise Sir, can *you* get the jewel from the lake?"

"I can try, Sire," replied Little Sage. "Let me stay and think a bit first."

And so the king and Big Sage and the rest of the men went to the king's tent, and left Little Sage by the lake. The slave girls had put golden bowls of fruit and sweetmeats in the tent for them; and soon one of them came down to the lake with her water jar to fetch water.

A stone made her slip; and Little Sage ran to help her. As he drew up her water pot, he saw the jewel shine in it. He stood still, for he saw two jewels now — one in the water pot, and one still in the lake.

He took the water pot up on to the bank and gave it to the slave girl. And now he saw no jewel in it.

So he went to the king's tent and told the king, "It will be no hard task, Sire, to get the jewel for you."

"I will come and see you do it," said the king.

And back he went to the lake with Little Sage, and all his men with him. Big Sage went, too.

"Well, how will you get it, Little Wise Sir?" asked the king.

"I will send a man up this tree, Sire," answered Little Sage.

And he put his hand on the trunk of a tree that grew on the bank of the lake, bent over the water.

Again Big Sage began to jeer, "Wise Little Sage! He will send a man up a tree to get a jewel that is below in the lake!"

"But the jewel is *not* below in the lake, Wise Sir," said Little Sage.

"Not in the lake?" cried the king. "But I can see it there!"

"Yet it is not in the lake, Sire," said Little Sage with a smile. "It is stuck fast among the twigs of a crow's nest in this tree. Send up a man, and he will soon bring it down to you."

So the king sent a man up the tree. As he put his hand in the crow's nest, the jewel in the lake vanished. The man came down with the jewel in his hand. He put it into the hand of Little Sage. Little Sage put it in turn into the hand of the king.

Then everyone around waved and cheered for Little Sage. And they all began to mock Big Sage: "Who made men dig and drain the lake to get the jewel that was up in the tree? O Wise Big Sage!"

Big Sage said to the king, "Sire, it has long been my wish to go up to the hills, and to be a hermit. Till you had a new sage to take my place, I felt I must stay with you. You have one now. So may I go now, Sire?"

"Go, Wise Sir, if that is your wish," said the king.

So Big Sage left the king, and Little Sage took his place. With his help, the king was able to rule the land well, and to part right from wrong and truth from lies as never before. Many a time, when they had seen Little Sage judge a case, the crowd cried out to him, "May you live long, Little Sage, to help poor men!"

And so he did.

# The Four Dangers

A good king stood one day at the gate of his palace. In the city street, he saw some boys catch a mouse. They held it up by the tail, and one of the boys took a knife from his waist.

"Boy, what is that knife for?" asked the king.

"Sire, to cut off the tail of this mouse," the boy told him.

"Let the mouse go," said the king. "Man is not man if he gives pain for the joy of it."

So the boys let the mouse go.

The mouse ran to the king and stood on his foot, and said, "O King, I owe you my thanks. To pay you, I will save your life one day."

"When will that be?" asked the king, with a smile.

And the mouse told him, "When your son is of age. A day will come when danger will lurk in the rice. You will see me then. When you see me, say this charm:

> *"Danger in the rice.*
> *Danger in the rice.*
> *Go, take it, and burn it!"*

"I will say it," said the king. And the mouse ran off.

Not long after this, the king was in his park. He liked to sit on a stone bench and look with joy on the trees and the birds and the deer.

As he sat there, a baby monkey fell from a high branch above. The king caught the small creature in his arms so that it was unhurt.

Then the mother swung down and said, "O King, I owe you my thanks for saving my baby's life. To pay you, I will save your life one day."

"When will that be?" asked the king, with a smile.

And the monkey told him, "When your son is of age. A day will come when danger will lurk in this tree. You will see me then. When you see me, say this charm:

*"Danger in the tree.*
*Danger in the tree.*
*I will not go near it."*

"I will say it," said the king. And the monkey sprang away with her infant into the trees.

A few days later, the king went to swim in his lotus lake. The fish were leaping with joy out of the still water. One fish leaped so high that it landed on the bank. It lay there shaking and unable to save itself.

The king came out of the water and gently picked up the fish. He put it back in the water.

Then the fish said to him, "O King, I owe you my thanks for saving my life. To pay you, I will save your life one day."

"When will that be?" asked the king, with a smile.

And the fish told him, "When your son is of age. A day will come when danger will lurk in this lake. You will see me then. When you see me, say this charm:

*"Danger in the lake.*
*Danger in the lake.*
*The lotus buds hide it."*

"I will say it," said the king. And the fish swam away.

Not long after this, a small bird fell from its nest on the roof of the palace, and hurt its wing. The king fed it in his room till it was able to fly.

As it spread its wings to fly back to its nest, the bird said, "O King, I owe you my thanks. To pay you, I will save your life one day."

"When will that be?" asked the king, with a smile.

And the bird told him, "When your son is of age. A day will come when danger will lurk in this bed. You will see me then. When you see me, say this charm:

*"Danger in the bed.*
*Danger in the bed.*
*Come forth, you who lie there!"*

"I will say it," said the king, with a smile. "But can you tell me how many more dangers lie in wait for me?"

"This will be the last danger to your life," said the bird. "If I save you this time, you will live to be old."

And with that, the bird flew away.

The years went by, and the king's son grew up. He began to long to be king in the place of his father.

"Must I wait to be king till I am old?" he said. "No; I will find some way to kill him."

So one day, when he went at dusk to eat with the king, the prince took drug-dust with him.

The rice was carried to the table in a golden dish. As the dish stood in front of him, the prince slid the drug-dust into it.

As he did so, a mouse ran past the dish. He gave the

rice a flip with his tail, and sent a grain or two flying right out of the dish.

At this, the mouse-charm came back to the king's mind, and he cried aloud:

*"Danger in the rice.*
*Danger in the rice.*
*Go, take it, and burn it!"*

A slave took the golden dish away to burn the rice. And the prince said in his own mind, "Did he see me put in the drug-dust? If he did not, then how did he know? And if he did, what will he do to me?"

The prince felt too afraid to eat. So he rose, made his bow to the king, and went out.

But time went on, and the king was still kind to his son, and as fond of him as ever. So the prince grew bold, and began to plot again to kill him.

He asked him one day, "My father, what will you do today?"

"I shall go to my park," said the king, "to hear the birds sing."

So the prince went out in haste, so that he got to the park first. He took his bow and arrows, and he hid in a tall tree near the stone bench where the king liked to sit. It was from the same tree that the baby monkey fell many years before.

As the king drew near to the tree, a monkey sprang out of it, then swung away. At this, the monkey-charm came back into the king's mind, and he cried aloud:

*"Danger in the tree.*
*Danger in the tree.*
*I will not go near it."*

And the king went away.

The prince hid in the tree till all was still in the park. Then he slid down to the ground, and sped back to the palace.

"Did he see me in the tree with my bow?" he said in his own mind. "If he did not, then how did he know? And if he did, what will he do to me?"

But time went on, and the king was still kind to his son, and as fond of him as ever. So the prince grew bold, and began yet again to plot to kill him.

He asked him one day, "My father, what will you do today?"

"I shall go and bathe in my lotus lake," said the king.

So the prince went out in haste, so that he got to the lotus lake first. He lay in the lake with a lotus leaf over his head, and with lotus buds in front of his face.

He had a silk cord in his hand. His plan was to wait till the king swam near, then to throw the cord around him and pull him under the water.

The king went down to the lake and began to swim. As he came near the lotus buds, a fish sprang out of the water and fell back with a splash.

At this, the fish-charm came back into the king's mind, and he cried aloud:

> "Danger in the lake.
> Danger in the lake.
> The lotus buds hide it."

The king put out his hand to part the lotus buds, and to see who hid among them. But with a deep dive, the prince got away. Only the silk cord still lay on a lotus leaf.

The prince was afraid. "Did he see me in the lake with my cord?" he said to himself. "If he did not, then how did he know? And if he did, what will he do to me?"

But time went on, and the king was still kind to his son, and as fond of him as ever. So the prince grew bold, and began yet again to plot to kill him.

He asked him one day, "My father, what will you do today?"

"It is hot," said the king. "At noon I shall go and rest."

So the prince took his sword, and went to the king's room on an upper floor of the palace. He lay down under the king's bed, his sword in his hand. His plan was to kill the king when he slept.

But as the king came into the room, a small bird flew in, and began to flit to and fro over the king's bed. At this, the bird-charm came back into the king's mind, and he cried aloud:

> *"Danger in the bed.*
> *Danger in the bed.*
> *Come forth, you who lie there!"*

Out came the prince. He fell on his face, to clasp his father's feet.

"My father, do not put me to death," he cried. "I vow that never again will I seek to kill you."

The king felt as if his heart would split in two.

"I love him; he is my son," one part of him said.

"But will he keep that vow?" said the other part.

Then it came into his mind that the bird had said, "This will be the last danger to your life. If I save you this time, you will live to be old."

So now the king bent to lift the prince up.

"You do your part, my son, and I will do mine," he said.

And this they both did. The prince from then on lived as the good son of a good father. And the king lived, much loved by his people, to a ripe old age.

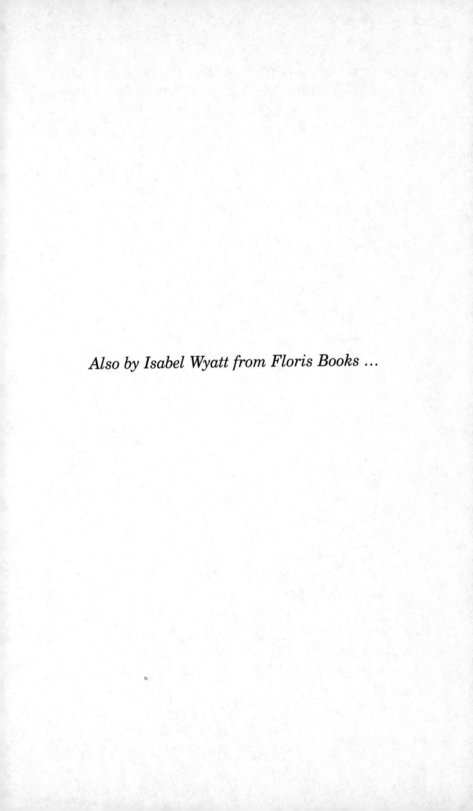

*Also by Isabel Wyatt from Floris Books ...*

When the king's son found gems in his horse's mane, he wondered, and still held his peace. But that night he withdrew early from the feast and hid himself in the shadows of the stable. Presently in came Cordita, her beauty shining through her rags ...

These magical tales take us through the highlights of the year, through festivals and birthdays.

With the wise counsel of the Golden Fish, the Fisher Boy sets out to win the heart of a beautiful princess. But first he must travel far and wide to find a golden eagle, a leaf-green bull, and a lion with a snow-white heart. Only then can he fight with a shining sword to conquer the dragon, fearsome beyond imagining.

A magical collection of beautifully-told stories which transport us to ivory towers, great forests, golden lands and kingdoms of beautiful colours.

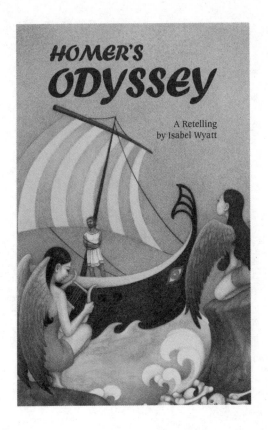

Homer's Odyssey is one of the greatest stories in literature, the epic tale of the return of Odysseus to his home following the Trojan war.

After nine years of siege and fighting, the Greeks are finally returning home. But one of the Greek heroes, Odysseus, offends the Sea-God, who sends storms and waves to keep him from arriving home for ten years. In this thrilling story, we follow Odysseus's trials and adventures as he faces one danger after another on his long journey.

The Vikings were the world's greatest adventurers and under-
took astonishing journeys recorded in the ancient sagas.

In these tales, the hero Thorkill of Iceland is sent by King
Gorm of Denmark on an dangerous mission to the land of Giants,
a journey his enemies plan he will never return from.